I'M NO TURKEY!

No part of this publication may be reproduced, stored in
a retrieval system, or transmitted in any form or by any means, electronic,
mechanical, photocopying, recording, or otherwise, without written permission
of the publisher. For more information regarding permission, write to
Scholastic Inc., 557 Broadway, New York, NY 10012.

Library of Congress Cataloging-in-Publication Data is available.

Copyright © 2008 by Hans Wilhelm, Inc.

All rights reserved. Published by Scholastic Inc.
SCHOLASTIC, CARTWHEEL BOOKS, NOODLES, and associated logos
are trademarks and/or registered trademarks of Scholastic Inc.
Lexile is a registered trademark of MetaMetrics, Inc.

ISBN-13: 978-0-545-07077-5
ISBN-10: 0-545-07077-5

12 11 10 9 8 7 6 5 4 3 2   10 11 12 13 14/0

Printed in the U.S.A.   40
This edition first printing, September 2009

BEGINNING READER

LEVEL 1

50-250 WORDS

I'M NO TURKEY!

by Hans Wilhelm

Cartwheel
·B·O·O·K·S· ®

SCHOLASTIC INC.

New York   Toronto   London   Auckland   Sydney
Mexico City   New Delhi   Hong Kong   Buenos Aires

It's Thanksgiving!

DING-DONG!

I'll get the door.

Welcome, everybody!

What are we making?

That looks like fun!
Can I help?

Hey, why are you
looking at me?

What is that?

What are you doing?
Stop it!

I'm no turkey!

You better not
laugh at me.

I won't wear feathers.
Off they go.

I know what
I'll do.

I *can* wear feathers.
I'll be a proud chief.

Now I can lead the parade.

Someone else can be
the Thanksgiving turkey.